The Tiara Club

at Ruby Mansions

D0333921

For the truly delightful Princess Anna,
daughter of wonderful Queen Janet
VF

With very special thanks to JD

www.tiaraclub.co.uk

ORCHARD BOOKS
338 Euston Road, London NW1 3BH
Orchard Books Australia
Level 17/207 Kent St, Sydney, NSW 2000

A Paperback Original
First published in Great Britain in 2007
Text © Vivian French 2007
Cover illustration © Sarah Gibb 2007
Illustrations © Orchard Books 2007

A CIP catalogue record for this book is available
from the British Library.

ISBN 978 1 84616 292 3

3 5 7 9 10 8 6 4 2

Printed in China

The paper and board used in this paperback are natural
recyclable products made from wood grown in sustainable
forests. The manufacturing processes conform to the
environmental regulations of the country of origin.

Orchard Books is a division of Hachette Children's Books
www.orchardbooks.co.uk

The Tiara Club
at Ruby Mansions

Princess Georgia

and the Shimmering Pearl

By Vivian French

ORCHARD BOOKS

The Royal Palace Academy
for the Preparation of Perfect Princesses

(Known to our students as "*The Princess Academy*")

OUR SCHOOL MOTTO:
*A Perfect Princess always thinks of others
before herself, and is kind, caring and truthful.*

Ruby Mansions offers a complete education for
Tiara Club princesses with emphasis on the
creative arts. The curriculum includes:

*Innovative Ideas for our
Friendship Festival*

*Ballet for Grace
and Poise*

*Designing Floral
Bouquets
(all thorns will be
removed)*

*A visit to the Diamond
Exhibition
(on the joyous occasion of
Queen Fabiola's birthday)*

Our headteacher, Queen Fabiola, is present at all times,
and students are well looked after by the head fairy
godmother, Fairy G, and her assistant, Fairy Angora.

Our resident staff and visiting experts include:

*KING BERNARDO IV
(Ruby Mansions Governor)*

*LADY HARRIS
(Secretary to Queen Fabiola)*

*LADY ARAMINTA
(Princess Academy Matron)*

*QUEEN MOTHER MATILDA
(Etiquette, Posture and
Flower Arranging)*

We award tiara points to encourage our Tiara Club princesses towards the next level. All princesses who win enough points at Ruby Mansions will attend a celebration ball, where they will be presented with their Ruby Sashes.

Ruby Sash Tiara Club princesses are invited to go on to Pearl Palace, our very special residence for Perfect Princesses, where they may continue their education at a higher level.

PLEASE NOTE:
Princesses are expected to arrive at
the Academy with a *minimum* of:

Twenty ballgowns
(with all necessary hoops,
petticoats, etc)

Twelve day dresses

Seven gowns
suitable for garden parties,
and other special
day occasions

Twelve tiaras

Dancing shoes
five pairs

Velvet slippers
three pairs

Riding boots
two pairs

Cloaks, muffs, stoles, gloves
and other essential
accessories as required

Hello – and I'm very pleased to meet you!
I'm Princess Georgia, and Chloe, Jessica,
Olivia, Lauren and Amy share Poppy
Room with me – and we're very best
friends. We're trying to be REAL
Perfect Princesses, but – guess what!
It isn't always easy!
I'm so glad you're here at Ruby Mansions
with us – but do watch out for the
horrible twins, Diamonde and Gruella.
They're SO mean.
But we'll look after you.
You're our friend!

Chapter One

Chloe started sneezing first. She sneezed twice over breakfast, and about fifty times during our first lesson, which was *Velvet Trains and How to Wear Them*, and by lunchtime she just couldn't stop. And her nose kept running and her eyes were red and she looked ghastly. POOR Chloe.

"I thig I'd better tell Fairy G I'b dot feeling very well," she said.

Of course Fairy G took Chloe STRAIGHT to Ruby Pillows, which is where we go if we're ill. It's a lovely light airy room up at the top of Ruby Mansions, and we

don't mind being there at all, even though Lady Araminta is VERY strict. She's the matron in charge of Ruby Pillows. Fairy G (our school Fairy Godmother) comes to visit a lot as well, and to check that everything's all right.

It's weird – you'd think a fairy godmother would just wave her wand and make everyone better, but she won't. She says it's cheating, and a waste of good magic.

By the middle of the afternoon Lauren was sneezing as well, and that night there were only four of us in Poppy Room – Amy, Jessica, Olivia and me. The others were tucked up with hot water bottles in Ruby Pillows, sniffing and snuffling and feeling miserable.

"Do you think I might catch it next?" Jessica asked hopefully as she climbed into bed. "There's that beastly test tomorrow, and I just KNOW I'm going to fail. I'll NEVER be able to *Design a Floral Bouquet to Present to a Very Special Princess* – but if I catch the bug I'll miss it!"

Olivia giggled. "'Now, princesses

– please remember that a Perfect Princess NEVER makes a mistake, and ALWAYS knows how to spell Variegated Nasturtiums!'"

Olivia is SO clever – she sounded exactly like Queen Mother Matilda! We all laughed, but my laugh turned into a sneeze.

"Oops!" I said, and fished under

my pillow for a hankie. "Maybe it'll be me that misses the test."

Jessica made a face at me. "That's not fair. You're sure to pass – you're BRILLIANT at flower arranging."

"You're the best of all of us," Amy told me, and she giggled. "It makes the twins SO jealous!"

Olivia nodded. "Diamonde went absolutely purple after it was your turn to do the flowers for assembly, and I'm sure Gruella tried to knock the vases over."

"She did," I said, "Atchoo! ATCHOOOO!"

Amy looked at me anxiously.

"Do you feel ill? Do you want me to get Fairy G?"

I shook my head. "I'll be OK for tonight," I said, although I was beginning to feel a bit woozy.

But by the morning I felt terrible, and I didn't even manage to wish the others good luck before Fairy G whisked me away to Ruby Pillows...

But none of us took part in the competition. When I woke up later on that morning and looked round, I saw every bed was full. All six of us from Poppy Room were there, and the twins, Diamonde and Gruella, were too.

"I feel TERRIBLE!" Diamonde wailed.

"You're not as bad as I am," Gruella told her. "I feel DREADFUL!"

"That's why you're here," Lady

Araminta said crisply, and she tucked in Diamonde and Gruella's covers so tightly they could hardly breathe.

Chapter Two

For the first couple of days we all felt too ill to talk very much, but on the third day I woke up feeling LOADS better. Lady Araminta came to take my temperature, and nodded.

"Excellent. We'll keep you here for a day or two more, just in case, but you're doing very nicely.

Now, you can get out of bed if you feel well enough, but you are NOT to go running around about disturbing everyone else!"

"Yes, Lady Araminta," I murmured.

Olivia was in the next bed, and she smiled at me. "Do you want to play a game?" she asked. "Fairy G came in when you were asleep yesterday, and left us some cards."

"Lovely," I said, and I hopped out of bed. "And no lessons for two days! Hurrah!"

Olivia shook her head. "Don't get too happy. Fairy G said she and Queen Mother Matilda were going to check on us this evening to see if we were well enough to do our designs for the floral bouquets tomorrow!"

I was HORRIFIED. "You mean,

do the test here in Ruby Pillows? While we're still ill?"

Lauren heard me, and came to sit on the edge of my bed. "Isn't it awful? And we can't even pretend we're worse than we are, because Fairy G ALWAYS knows if you're ill or not."

I nodded. That's the trouble with fairy godmothers. They're just too clever. "Oh well," I said, "we'd better enjoy ourselves while we can." And we settled down to a game of Snap.

By the time Fairy G arrived that evening, I was back in bed. It's funny how one minute you can feel TOTALLY better, and the next your legs go wobbly, and it's actually rather nice to be lying back on soft snow-white pillows.

Fairy G swooped into the room and beamed at us, and Queen Mother Matilda sailed in after her.

"Now, my dears," Fairy G boomed, "let's see how you're doing! Will you be well enough tomorrow to dazzle us all with your posies of roses? Or will you still be a bunch of faded flowers?"

"I'm sure they'll be QUITE all right," Queen Mum Mattie snapped. "A Perfect Princess must always continue with her duties, regardless of her personal circumstances." She SO didn't think Fairy G was funny.

Fairy G didn't answer. She was hunting about in her enormous handbag, and she finally pulled out the most beautiful pearl on a long silver chain.

"I knew it was in there somewhere!" she said cheerfully.

"Does anyone think they're too poorly to do the test tomorrow?"

Gruella and Diamonde's hands shot in the air.

"H'm," Fairy G said, and she eyed them thoughtfully. "Let's see. This is my latest magical invention – it's a Truth Teller!"

And she set the pearl swinging round and round.

"Oooh!" I gasped. "It's FABULOUS!"

"It is pretty, isn't it?" Fairy G agreed. "Now, watch carefully..."

"Funny kind of magic if you ask me," Diamonde whispered to Gruella. "It would be more use if it made us better – but I suppose that would be MUCH too hard. Fairy G's only a SCHOOL Fairy Godmother, after all."

I saw Fairy G look at Diamonde, and I was certain she'd heard what she said, but she didn't tell her off. Instead she smiled.

"I'm afraid I can't make you better, my dears, but the pearl will tell me if you really are too poorly to do the test tomorrow."

We stared at the pearl, and as it went on circling round and round it stopped shimmering, and turned grey.

"Everyone's fine." Fairy G gave Diamonde and Gruella a brisk nod, and dropped the pearl back in her bag.

Gruella began to groan. "But I feel hot all over, and my head's splitting."

"You'll be quite all right by tomorrow, Princess Gruella. Fairy G's magic is NEVER wrong." Queen Mother Matilda wasn't at all sympathetic. "We'll see you in the morning." And she and Fairy G hurried out of the dormitory.

A moment later Fairy G popped her head back round the door. "Don't forget, my dears, there's a LOVELY prize for the winner, and all her friends as well!" And she smiled, and disappeared.

We stared at each other after Fairy G had gone. "A lovely prize for what?" Chloe asked.

"A prize for whoever does the best bouquet, of course," Diamonde sneered. She gave me a cold look. "And we all know who thinks they're going to win!"

I shrugged, and snuggled down in my bed. "We'll see what happens tomorrow," I said. "Goodnight!"

Chapter Three

I woke up early the following morning, and I felt amazing! I hopped out of bed, and after I'd collected a piece of paper and pencils from Lady Araminta's store cupboard, I began drawing and colouring ideas for bouquets. I absolutely LOVE flowers – my parents have got the hugest palace garden ever – and when I was little I spent all day with the head gardener.

I hadn't been drawing for long when I had an idea. I decided I'd use lots of flowers like pale blue Love-in-a-Mist, and the palest mauve and pink sweet peas and white Baby's Breath – so the bouquet would look very delicate – and then I'd have trailing ivy mixed with the sweetest pale pink and mauve ribbons.

I was really enjoying myself when I suddenly noticed Gruella was staring over my shoulder.

"What's THAT stuff?" she

asked. "That fluffy stuff?"

I SO wanted to hide my picture because I had a nasty feeling Gruella might copy my idea, but *Perfect Princesses Always Think the Best of Others*. I sighed, and told her it was Love-in-a-Mist.

"I'M going to make my bouquet with PROPER flowers," Gruella said snootily. "Roses and lilies!" She pointed to my drawing of sweet peas. "Are those things meant to be butterflies? That's silly. They'll fly away."

Before I could answer, Lady Araminta came sweeping into Ruby Pillows, clapping her hands to wake everyone up.

"No time for scribbling now, Princess Georgia," she told me as Gruella scurried off. I hastily folded my drawing, and pushed it under my pillow.

"We've a busy morning ahead of

us," Lady Araminta went on, "and I want everything neat and tidy before Queen Mother Matilda arrives. And – " Lady A looked VERY pleased – "we have the most delightful surprise! Your headteacher, Queen Fabiola, has decided to come to Ruby Pillows and judge your designs!"

She so obviously expected us to be totally thrilled I began to clap. After a second or two everyone else joined in, and Lady A smiled approvingly.

"Quite right. Queen Fabiola has already looked at all the drawings that Rose Room, Lavender Room and the others did yesterday. Now it's your turn. Please make your beds, and go to Ruby Pillows dining room for breakfast. Once you have finished, the dining tables will be cleared, and paper and colouring pens set out for your test."

There was a lot of chatting about ideas over breakfast, but Diamonde and Gruella didn't join in. Instead, they kept whispering to each other. As soon as Queen Mother Matilda arrived they rushed up to her, and curtsied.

"Please, Your Majesty," Diamonde said with her best smile, "PLEASE may we work together? We've had SUCH a lovely idea!"

"That's right." Gruella curtsied again. "And we'd like to call it the Queen Mother Matilda Bouquet, in honour of you!"

Queen Mother Mattie looked

thoughtful. "Well..." she began, "it is meant to be a bouquet for a Very Special Princess..."

"PLEASE," Diamonde begged, and she smiled a horrible sickly smile.

"Very well, my dears." Queen Mother Matilda handed them a sheet of paper, and they hurried back to their table and started drawing at once.

"I'm truly delighted to see that at least two of you have prepared for this test," the Queen Mother said as she put the pile of drawing paper down. "The rest of you, begin as soon as you are ready – and DON'T forget to put your names on your designs!"

Two minutes later, the dining room was very quiet as we began to sketch out our ideas.

After a while Queen Mother Matilda began walking round and peering over our shoulders, and I saw her nodding in a pleased kind of way as she looked at Gruella and Diamonde's drawing.

"Charming!" she said, "really charming!"

She moved on to Olivia, and then Jessica, and on down the length of the table. By the time she reached me I had nearly finished, and though I know it's TERRIBLE to boast, I was quite pleased with what I'd done. I waited for Queen Mother Mattie to nod at me too, but she didn't. She stood very still, and gave me the most FREEZING stare.

"Princess Georgia," she said, "this is NOT what I would expect from a Perfect Princess."

I stared at her in amazement. Whatever did she mean?

Queen Mother Mattie made an

angry tut-tutting noise, and frowned at me. "We'll have to see what Queen Fabiola has to say about this, Georgia. And if I'm not much mistaken, she's just arrived!"

The Queen Mother was right.

A trumpeter leapt into the dining room, and blew a loud "TAN TARA TARA!". When he had finished, he bowed, and stood back to allow Queen Fabiola and Fairy G to come stumping past him.

Fairy G was rubbing her ears. "MUST he do that quite so loudly?" she grumbled.

Queen Fabiola waved her ear trumpet. "But it's such FUN, Fairy G! And I can hear it beautifully!" She beamed round at all of us. "You think it's fun, don't you, my dears?"

We curtsied deeply, and said, "Yes, Your Majesty," although our ears were ringing.

"Excellent! Excellent!" Our headteacher beamed at us. "And now let's see these lovely pictures for beautiful bouquets. Rose Room and the others did very

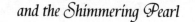

well, and I'm longing to see what you've been up to."

Queen Mother Matilda stepped forward, still holding my design.

"One moment, Your Majesty," she said, and she sounded SO serious. "We have a problem." And she handed Queen Fabiola my piece of paper.

Chapter Four

My heart started pitter-pattering in my chest as I watched Queen Fabiola turn my picture the right way up.

"But this is WONDERFUL!" she said as she studied it.

Queen Mother Matilda shook her head. "Princess Gruella! Princess Diamonde! Please bring your picture here," she ordered.

Gruella and Diamonde came skipping up, and curtsied. They fluttered their eyelashes at Queen Fabiola, and Gruella murmured, "We're SO honoured to show you our little idea, Your Majesty."

But Diamonde was peeping at the piece of paper in Queen Fabiola's hand.

"OH!" she SQUEALED, and threw her arms in the air. "Gruella! LOOK! Do look! Georgia's copied OUR design!"

And she gave me SUCH a triumphant stare that I just knew they'd planned exactly what they were going to do and say.

Queen Fabiola looked at the two pictures. They did look almost exactly the same.

"I'm afraid there's no doubt that Georgia is guilty," Queen Mother Matilda told our headteacher. "The twins began drawing long before anyone else."

"That's right," Gruella said smugly. "We did, didn't we, Diamonde? So that PROVES Georgia is a cheat!"

"Just one moment!" It was Fairy G, and her voice was sharp. "I think Princess Georgia should be allowed to say how she believes this strange coincidence has happened."

I looked at Fairy G gratefully, but it was difficult to know what to say without being a horrible telltale. I bobbed another little curtsey, and said, "I'm afraid I can't explain. I did a sketch for my idea early on before breakfast, and then I drew it again for the competition... that's all."

"She's lying!" Diamonde interrupted. "She copied us! I know she did!"

"SILENCE!" When Fairy G is angry she grows HUGE, and looks really scary.

She towered above us all, and even Queen Fabiola looked taken aback.

"Can you show us this sketch?"

Fairy G asked me. Even though she was looking angry, she sounded quite kind.

I was about to say I didn't know where it was – and then I remembered!

"Yes!" I said. "I pushed it under my pillow..."

Queen Mother Matilda began to huff and to puff. "Surely there's no need for this, Fairy G," she

complained. "It seems to me it's a cut and dried case of cheating!"

Fairy G opened her bag, pulled out her wonderful pearl, and set it swinging round and round – and I gasped. It wasn't pearl coloured any more – it was BLACK!

"SOMEONE is not telling the truth," she said, and she turned to Lady Araminta. "Dear Lady A, would you be so kind as to look under Georgia's pillow?"

Lady A hurried off. My heart began to thump louder and louder...supposing my picture wasn't there after all? But a moment later she was back, with my crumpled drawing in her hand.

"Actually," she said, "I did see Princess Georgia busy drawing this morning. She was with Princess Gruella, just before breakfast."

Fairy G nodded, and hung the pearl over my drawing. At once it cleared, and began to shimmer in the most GORGEOUS way. Fairy G nodded again, and held the pearl over Diamonde and Gruella's picture...and first it went a nasty green, and then gradually darkened to black.

There was a long silence, and then Gruella began to whimper. "We didn't REALLY copy Georgia's picture. I must have just sort of noticed it when I was asking about the flowers..."

"That's right," Diamonde agreed. "We must have copied it by mistake."

Queen Fabiola lifted up her ear trumpet. "What? What's that you're saying, child? A mistake? Who's made a mistake?"

"I think the Princesses Gruella and Diamonde have made a mistake, Your Majesty," Fairy G said, and she sounded grim.

"A very unpleasant mistake."
Diamonde looked at Gruella,
and Gruella looked at Diamonde.

They went bright red, and then Diamonde said, all in one breath, "We're very very sorry if it looked as if Georgia copied our picture because she didn't and we didn't mean to make ours the same but it just happened that way because we're so ILL." And she grabbed Gruella's hand, and they bolted out of the Ruby Pillows dining room. Chloe was nearest the door, and she told me later that she saw them dive into their beds, and pull their duvets right up over their heads.

"I think," Fairy G said calmly, "we'll leave the twins to think about what they've done."

Queen Mother Matilda looked flustered. "Do I understand it was the *twins* who were cheating?" she asked. She patted me on the head. "Oh dear me! I'm so sorry, Georgia. I was MUCH too hasty in my judgement!"

"I'm sure Princess Georgia will forgive you," Queen Fabiola said. "After all, there's no doubt in my mind that she's won the prize for the most beautiful bouquet. Fairy G, could I ask you to wave your magic wand?"

Chapter Five

I didn't know where to look.
Everything had happened so
suddenly – instead of being in
disgrace, I was the winner!
I'd won the prize! And as
Fairy G waved her wand, flowers
began to fall from the ceiling...
and they were all the flowers
I had chosen.

"Come along, Poppy Room!" Fairy G gave us a huge smile. "Georgia will tell you what to do! We want to see each of you make the most beautiful bouquet..."

And we did. I do think Fairy G must have added a little extra fairy dust, though, because the flowers almost flew into the right places, and the ribbons curled themselves into the loveliest loops and twirls. In no time at all we were each holding the most GORGEOUS bouquet – and I'm not being boastful. Truly. The flowers were so very VERY pretty, and Fairy G's magic had given them an extra sparkle.

Queen Fabiola smiled at us. "There!" she said. "Six beautiful bouquets – for six Very Special Princesses! And I think you'll find that they last for a long LONG time...isn't that right, Fairy G?"

Fairy G nodded. "They certainly will," she said. "Oh, and there's just one last thing I have to do..." She took the pearl, and began to twirl it round and round and round again. Gradually it began to shimmer, and to glow, until it was as lovely as it had been when we first saw it.

"Excellent!" Fairy G said. "Although I think the poor thing is almost worn out. Let me try one last twirl..."

And it was AMAZING!!

Hanging up behind our chairs were just the most adorable pearl-coloured dresses you could ever imagine...and the sashes were pale pink, and blue, and mauve, to match the flowers in our bouquets.

We looked at each other with wide eyes.

"THANK YOU!" we breathed. "They're WONDERFUL!"

"I told you there was a prize," Fairy G said. "But that's quite enough excitement for now! You'll be back in Ruby Mansions tomorrow...so enjoy today, and NO rushing around!"

"I'LL make sure of that," Lady

Araminta said firmly. "And now I think it's time for a little rest."

Queen Fabiola looked surprised. "Best?" she said. "Best? But we know who's best! It's Poppy Room! Didn't I just tell them?"

And we couldn't help laughing...

*

As Lady Araminta tucked us into our beds that night, I peeped at our bouquets on our bedside tables and I couldn't help thinking how LUCKY I was to be at Ruby Mansions...and I'm so lucky my friends are here too...especially you.

What happens next?
Find out in

and the Velvet Cloak

Hello! I'm Princess Olivia,
one of the Poppy Room Princesses,
and I'm so pleased you're here too.
Maybe you know Chloe, Jessica, Georgia,
Lauren and Amy? They're my best
friends, and they're LOVELY! Not at all
like the twins, Diamonde and Gruella.
I know Perfect Princesses shouldn't
be mean about other princesses,
but those two are SO horrid.

Look out for

Butterfly Ball

with Princess Amy and Princess Olivia!
ISBN 978 1 84616 470 5

*And look out for the Lily Room princesses in
the Tiara Club at Pearl Palace:*

Princess Hannah and the Little Black Kitten
Princess Isabella and the Snow-White Swan
Princess Lucy and the Precious Puppy
Princess Grace and the Golden Nightingale
Princess Ellie and the Enchanted Fawn
Princess Sarah and the Silver Swan

By Vivian French
Illustrated by Sarah Gibb

The Tiara Club

The Tiara Club at Silver Towers

The Tiara Club at Ruby Mansions

All priced at £3.99.
Christmas Wonderland and *Butterfly Ball* are priced at £5.99.
The Tiara Club books are available from all good bookshops, or can be ordered direct
from the publisher: Orchard Books, PO BOX 29, Douglas IM99 IBQ.
Credit card orders please telephone 01624 836000 or fax 01624 837033 or visit our
website: www.wattspub.co.uk or e-mail: bookshop@enterprise.net for details.

To order please quote title, author, ISBN and your full name and address.
Cheques and postal orders should be made payable to 'Bookpost plc.'
Postage and packing is FREE within the UK
(overseas customers should add £2.00 per book).

Prices and availability are subject to change.

Check out

The
Tiara
Club

website at:

www.tiaraclub.co.uk

You'll find Perfect Princess games and fun things to do, as well as news on the Tiara Club and all your favourite princesses!